CRICKET AND THE EMPEROR'S SON

Other books by Elizabeth Coatsworth

Cricket
and
the Emperor's Son

By

ELIZABETH   COATSWORTH

Drawings by

JULIETTE   PALMER

W · W · NORTON & COMPANY · INC ·

New York

To Catherine
in her osier basket

1298156

CONTENTS

CRICKET AND THE EMPEROR'S SON

Once upon a time there lived in Japan a widowed mother and her son, whom she called the Cricket, because he was small for his age and cheerful and home-loving They were poor farmers and all day they worked together in the rice terraces, often up to their knees in water as they stooped over the young plants. Or Cricket would plough with a great water buffalo borrowed from a neighbour, and then his mother, guiding the patient animal with her shrill cries, admired his dexterity, as, small as he was, he clung bravely to the unwieldy plough and drove it deep into the dark earth. But when the long day's work was done they loved to sit together, eating their meagre dinner and gazing out across the sloping rice terraces to the valley below them, through which ran a stream laced with willow trees.

Cricket loved then to have his mother tell him stories: tales of the snake that lived in the corner of the garden when she was a little girl and had offerings made to it, or of the foxes that carry the messages of the harvest god through the summer rice and dance with green flames on the tips of their noses, or of the wars of the Samurai, the warriors who carry two swords and must never show fear.

One evening his mother said to him:

"As you know, we are only farmers and come of humble stock. Yet in your veins, too, runs Samurai blood. Long ago when my grandmother was a young girl, a wounded Samurai came to the village, and was hidden away in our loft until the search for him was over. My grandmother tended him and, as he was a ruined man with no place to go and no hope to guide him, he remained in the village and married the young girl who had served him. He did not live long. His pride and his wounds gave him no rest. But it has always seemed to me that you must be very like him, for you are braver and gentler than the other village boys, you see beauty where they see nothing, and there is something in your way of walking and the oval of your face that does not come from the fields."

She was silent for a while, and Cricket, too, was

silent, for his thoughts were hushed by surprise at his mother's praise and this story of noble blood. After a while he heard her voice again, quieter than ever:

"I tell you this because tomorrow I am sending you away. Your uncle has arranged for you to be apprenticed to a friend of his, a silk merchant, in the capital. Be diligent and obedient to your master, and who knows? Perhaps you may prosper, too, and be a merchant with your own shop!" She clapped her hands softly. "Oh, the things you will see and hear in the great city!" she added wistfully. "I do not wish you to half starve always on this hillside."

"But what will you do without me, honourable mother?" asked Cricket, feeling very young and alone at the idea of leaving all he had ever known and going away among strangers.

"Your uncle will help me," said his mother, and so the matter was arranged.

It was not until towards evening of the next day that Cricket met his new master. All the silk shops were on the same street, and Cricket's country eyes and ears and nose were assailed by the crowds and the clamour and the smell of dyes, but he walked at

9

his uncle's side as though he had always known such things. If only he could suddenly be at home, sitting with his mother, telling her of all he had seen! But he must keep an untroubled face and a cheerful look.

This was not easy after he had seen his master, a fat heavy-necked man jesting over the saké cups with his uncle, while they arranged the terms of his apprenticeship: food and a winter kimono and a summer kimono and mats in the garret for Cricket, and in return his loyal services and obedience in all things. And after long, long years of servitude a share in the business.

The silk merchant's shadow danced large and thick as an ogre's on the wall. His heavy voice was jovial now, but there was a sound in it like the grumble of tides among unseen rocks when all the sky is blue. With a heavy heart, but still smiling, Cricket said farewell to his uncle and climbed the steep stairs to the draughty loft where he was to sleep. Even by himself in the dark, he kept on smiling, driving back the fear and loneliness about him with calm thoughts. Did he not have Samurai blood, although he was only little Cricket, the apprentice? He must succeed so that his mother might rest when she was old. She should sit by a brazier in a warm robe and have all she wanted to eat and a little maid-servant to wait upon her.

Resolutely smiling, Cricket fell asleep.

All next day he kept cheerful and the next and the next, and as the weeks went by and the months, they found Cricket smiling still, no matter what happened to him. He had not been mistaken about his master. The silk merchant was as ready with a blow as with a word, and gave blame more easily than praise. At dawn his harsh bellow woke Cricket among his thin mats. All day the boy served customers, or ran errands about the great city, often carrying bolts of silk too heavy for his thin shoulders. His food was as scanty as it had been on the farm, and was eaten hastily without the sauce of love. But Cricket never faltered, and his dark observant eyes saw everything that went on about him and weighed it in his mind. Was it beautiful? Was it honourable? Perhaps he had been beaten that morning, but his heart leaped none the less at the bravery of a procession of some great lord come to town with his retainers and horses and pennons. Perhaps he was supperless, but he could still rejoice at the great flowers of the fireworks bursting over the roofs of the city during some festival. At the end of six months, he was thinner than ever, but his eyes were untroubled and gentle and he still walked with an unconscious dignity.

It happened about this time that his master decided to send Cricket to the priest in the nearby temple to learn how to read and write. In spite of himself he was impressed by Cricket's character, and knew that the keeping of the accounts would be safe in his hands.

"You lazy good-for-nothing!" he shouted at his apprentice one morning, "you are no more use here than an ape. I am going to see if you have wit enough to learn anything." And so with a box on the ear he took him to the priest.

From that time on Cricket had every day a refuge

from his troubled life. For an hour he might sit respectfully before the old quiet priest in a quiet room, listening to his priceless wisdom while the temple doves cooed softly among the eaves.

All that was fine in the boy found here a fineness to feed upon in the words of long-dead sages and poets. The priest was patient and wise. His old eyes saw how brave a spirit looked out at him from the face of the little overworked apprentice, and Cricket was quick to learn and his spirit was eager for beauty.

"Respect the written word," the priest told him one day. "The noblest thoughts have come to us through the humble instruments of brush and ink-slab and paper. Writing is sacred and should never be used for ignoble purposes. It is shameful to see a piece of paper that may have a beautiful idea on it blowing about in the mud and trodden underfoot."

From that moment Cricket picked up any piece of paper with writing on it which he saw in the streets and brought it to the temple to burn before the statue of the God of Writing. Sometimes he was delayed on his errands by chasing a wind-blown scrap of paper hither and yon.

"Why are you late?" his master asked him more than once, and when poor Cricket murmured:

"Excuse me, sir, there was a paper which the

wind kept blowing—" the silk merchant would box his ears and cry:

"What do I feed and keep you for? To go about collecting useless writing? No! and no! and no! How is writing going to help you? You'll end in a beggar's grave, you stupid boy!"

But that is where his master, who thought himself so wise, was wrong. For a paper and writing did help Cricket, all in good time.

One day the news spread about the city that the Emperor's only son was ill. The court physicians tried one medicine and then another. Sometimes people said the Prince was better and sometimes they said he was worse. It seemed that he was besieged by a demon of sleeplessness, which left him each morning weaker than he had been the day before, and no medicine or charm helped at all. The Emperor and Empress made offerings for his recovery at all the temples, and the people made offerings, and even poor Cricket took the few coppers he had, and bought a spray of flowers to lay before the altar of the God of Writing.

Not long afterwards as he was walking along a street with three bolts of silk on his tired shoulders, he suddenly came upon the ruins of a house that had

recently burned. Near it he saw a piece of paper, traced with writing such as men used in the olden days when writing was as beautiful as any picture. It seemed to have been torn from one of the smouldering books he saw near by.

Carefully laying down his load, Cricket picked up the paper and slipped it into the breast of his robe before hurrying on. He was so busy that he never thought of it again until he was going to bed in his garret. Then holding it near the bit of light he was allowed, he read what was written on it, which seemed to be the beginning of a story about China, that land from which so many legends have come to Japan. Just at the most exciting part of the story the page ended, and blowing out his light, Cricket lay down on his thin quilt to dream of the Emperor's son.

Next morning Cricket's master woke him as usual at dawn, shouting from his warm bed below. As he dressed, the boy took a moment to glance again at the page he had rescued. But what was this? The story began where it had ended the night before! As often as he finished reading, he had only to begin again to find the writing all new, while the story flowed on as smoothly as a river, and all on the one torn slip of paper. Cricket could scarcely believe his eyes!

"Are you coming down or shall I come up to get you?" roared his master in a rage from below, and Cricket hastily hid the wonderful piece of paper and hurried to his work. All morning he thought and thought, and in the afternoon when his master happened to be away he returned to his garret, washed himself carefully, smoothed his hair, brushed his mended garments, and putting the page again in his bosom, left the shop. His conscience troubled him somewhat, for well he knew the silk merchant would never have consented to his plan, but he weighed his duty to his master against his duty to the only son of his Emperor, and held bravely to his course.

He had often walked by the glorious gates of the palace on his errands, but the idea of passing through them had never occurred to him before. At any other time no one would have paid attention to a small unknown apprentice, but now, with the Prince so ill, everyone was at his wit's end to find help, and something in the steadiness of Cricket's glance and the simple way he told his story impressed the gatekeeper, who finally sent him to the Chancellor himself. The great man put on his Chinese spectacles (which had pink quartz instead of glass for lenses), read through the writing on the paper, and then with growing astonishment read through it again, and having made sure with his own eyes that the words had really changed right under his own nose, exclaimed:

"It is true that you are a person of no possible importance and should never come near the sacred person of the Prince, but the dry earth does not ask from which direction the rain comes, and the humblest being may be the mouth-piece of a god."

Then he ordered his attendants to dress Cricket suitably and lead him to the Prince's apartments that evening at the hour of the imperial Going-to-Bed.

For hours Cricket sat waiting. Sometimes he thought of his mother and wondered how things were with her. Sometimes he thought of the Emperor's son and prayed that he might be able to save the imperial boy from the demon of wakefulness that tormented him. But of himself he scarcely thought at all, nor of his master's rage if he, Cricket, should return to the silk shop after running away without his permission.

At last evening came and Cricket was led to the Prince's apartments. Cricket did not see the Prince, for a beautiful screen painted with chrysanthemums in a mist of gold was drawn between him and the royal child. Attendants sat here and there. One of these brought a light, and Cricket, bowing low towards the screen, said in a trembling voice:

"May it please your Exalted Highness to have your servant read from the magic paper he has with him?"

And from behind the screen a faint, tired voice replied: "Read."

So Cricket read the title, "Wang Li and the Princesses," which he found written in characters as graceful as narcissus flowers on their stems, and amid the silent attention of the courtiers he bowed once more low towards the screen and began.

WANG LI AND THE PRINCESSES

In my province there is a mountain. It is called the Mountain of the Seven Stars. It is a wonderful mountain. Dragons live in it. A great river flows about its feet. A lake like a mirror lies below it. There are forests, too, on its sides. It is a beautiful mountain. It is so beautiful that years ago a wise man came to live as a hermit in one of its caves. He looks out at all this beauty, at the forests, at the lake, at the great river below him and thinks. His thoughts, too, are beautiful.

There are farms in the valley. In the beginning they were little farms, for the people were poor.

In the farm nearest the mountain lived a young man with his mother. His name was Wang Li. Sometimes he climbed the mountain to carry a bowl of food to the hermit, which the hermit took from him in silence.

Wang Li was a young man. He was very handsome. He worked hard on his little farm. His mother was a widow and growing old. She did what she could to help her son.

Sometimes Wang Li fished in the river. Sometimes Wang Li hunted in the forests. He was a good fisherman and a good hunter. And so the pot on his mother's fire was seldom empty.

But one spring the rains did not come. The people waited and waited but still they did not come. The young rice began to die in the fields. The silkworms had little to eat. The waters in the river were low. Fish died in the shallow pools. The birds flew everywhere looking for food. Even the deer were hungry.

"Soon we shall starve," said Wang Li's mother.

"The hermit must be hungry," said Wang Li. "I will take him a bowl of rice."

"But we have not enough for ourselves," cried his mother.

"I am young. I will go without eating."

"No, we will share what we have," said his mother.

And when he was at the door, she touched his arm.

"I am proud that my son has a good heart," she said.

Wang Li climbed the mountain. The sky was clear and blue. Far off he thought he saw a flock of white swans flying.

The hermit was sitting in the sun in front of his cave. He said nothing as Wang Li put the bowl of food down beside him.

But as Wang Li turned to go he said, "A worthy man is only a worthy man in his own place."

Wang Li bowed low. He walked down the mountain, with his eyes on the ground. He was thinking of what the hermit had said.

But suddenly far off he heard a lovely sound. He looked up. The swans were near now. They were circling over the forest.

"They are going to Shadow Lake," he thought.

And he turned and made his way towards the lake.

Wang Li was a hunter. He went without sound. As he drew near he heard a babble of splashing water, of sweet cries, almost of laughter.

"The swans are playing on the lake," Wang Li thought.

But when he looked through the leaves, he did not see swans. Instead young girls were at play on the lake. They were as beautiful as swans, and as proud.

As he watched, the most beautiful of the young girls came near where he was hidden. He reached out and caught her by one white wing. At her cry the other girls flew up from the water. The air was loud with their wings.

"Who are you?" Wang Li asked.

"I am the youngest daughter of the Cloud Dragon. And if you will let me go, I will take you to my father's palaces. You shall be my husband, and a great prince."

"What should I do in your father's palaces?" said Wang Li. "A worthy man is only a worthy man in his own place."

"But you are handsome and young," said the swan princess. "Come with me. It is my wish."

"It is for you to come with me if you wish, then," said Wang Li. "My house is poor, but we will share what we have."

Then the swan princess wept. She was too proud to come to a poor man's house.

"Go then," said Wang Li. "But send rain to us so that we may live. And in the future do not forget us, and our fields."

Then the daughter of the Cloud Dragon flew

away to join her sisters. But her tears still fell. By the time Wang Li reached his own house the rain, too, was falling.

"Oh the spring rain! The spring rain!" cried his mother at the door. "We shall not starve after all!"

Later on, she said, "But why are you sad?"

"I saw a beautiful bird," said Wang Li, "and it flew away."

"That is nothing to be sad about," said his mother.

So the sun rose and the sun set, and one day followed another. The rain fell, neither too much nor too little. And all went well for Wang Li and his mother.

And often Wang Li took a bowl of food to the hermit, who accepted it in silence.

But later in the year, the river rose in a flood. It washed away the fields. It came nearer and nearer Wang Li's house.

"Now we shall all be drowned," cried his mother. "And just when things were going so well!"

Wang Li took his bow and arrows.

"Where are you off to?" asked his mother. "This is no time for hunting."

"There may be great game afoot," said Wang Li.

The young man walked along the rushing water

towards the Mountain of the Seven Stars. The water made a great roaring. Sometimes a whole tree or a piece of a broken bridge rushed past.

And then came something beautiful. A young girl on a white horse was riding on the rushing water. The feet of her white horse were hidden in the spray. Behind her followed other young girls on white horses. All were beautiful and proud.

Wang Li fitted an arrow to his bow string. He drew the bow. The arrow whistled and was gone. But there it hung in the young girl's head-dress of pearls, white as the spray.

She reached up and pulled it free. Then she rode to the bank where Wang Li stood.

"Who are you who shoots arrows at the youngest daughter of the River Dragon?" she asked.

"I am Wang Li, a poor man and the son of a poor man," replied Wang Li.

"I have never seen a man before," said the princess. "Since you have spared my life, you shall come back with me to my father's coral palaces. You shall marry me and be a prince."

"A worthy man is only a worthy man in his own place," said Wang Li. "Come with me to the little farm where I live with my mother. We will share what we have with you."

24

"I am a princess," said the young girl on the white horse, proudly.

"Then if you will not come, at least see that the river returns to its banks. Give back our fields to us. And in the future do us no more harm."

"It shall be as you wish," said the daughter of the River Dragon. Then she turned her horse and rode away, weeping.

When Wang Li reached home his mother met him at the door.

"Look!" she cried. "The river is going down. We are saved. And our fields will be rich with new earth carried from the mountain."

Later on she asked, "But why are you so sad?"

"I saw a beautiful fish," said Wang Li, "and it swam away."

"That is nothing to be sad about," said his mother.

So the sun rose and the sun set and one day followed another. The rain fell, neither too much nor too little. The river kept within its banks and all went well for Wang Li and his mother. And more often than ever Wang Li took his bowl of food to the hermit who sat at the door of his cave and said nothing.

But one day the earth began to shake. Wang Li's

little house rocked from side to side. The bowls fell off the shelf. The rafters creaked. Clay fell from the walls. Outside the trees swayed their crests. The rooster crowed and the chickens cackled in fear.

"We shall all be killed!" cried Wang Li's mother. "And just when things were going so well, too!"

Wang Li took up his spear.

"Where are you off to?" asked his mother. "This is no time to go hunting!"

"There may be great game afoot," said Wang Li.

The young man walked quickly towards the Mountain of the Seven Stars. It was hard to walk. The ground was heaving under his feet. The grasses sighed and tossed beside his path.

When he came to the foot of the mountain, he saw a long mound of earth, as though a giant mole had been burrowing.

"Ah ha, someone is walking here!" said Wang Li.

He stuck his spear deep into the earth.

"When he returns, he will scratch his back," said Wang Li.

He was about to go home again, but suddenly he heard a sound of weeping. There under a pine tree he saw a beautiful young girl spinning as she wept. She was dressed in old clothes, but Wang Li knew that she was a princess.

"Who are you?" he asked.

"I am Beautiful Jade, the youngest daughter of the Dragon of the Mountain," the girl replied through her tears. "My uncle has seized my father's kingdom. He has imprisoned him in the deepest cavern, and rules in his place. Me he has driven out from my father's palace. I live on roots and berries. And I must spin all day for my living."

"Will you return with me to my little farm?" asked Wang Li. "My mother and I will share with you what we have."

"I will gladly go with you," said the princess.

All this time the earth had been rumbling and shaking. Suddenly it gave a great shake. Wang Li and the princess were thrown to the ground. Great trees were broken off like sticks. Birds flew about with wild cries.

Then all was still.

"I think your uncle must have walked into my spear," said Wang Li, helping Beautiful Jade to her feet.

"Then my father will once more be Dragon King," said she. "If you will come with me to his golden palace——"

But Wang Li said, "A worthy man is only worthy in his own place."

The princess thought about this in silence.

"That is very wise," she said at last. "I will go with you, then, to your house since that is your place."

So Beautiful Jade went with Wang Li, and they were married. And the young princess worked hard like the other farm women. In every way she tried to please Wang Li's mother and Wang Li's mother loved her, as if she were her own daughter. And when a little son was born, their happiness was complete.

And the sun rose, and the sun set and day followed day. And the rains came in their season. And the river kept within its banks. And everything prospered on Wang Li's farm until he had buffaloes and pigs and herd boys in the fields and women in the house to help his mother and Beautiful Jade. Nor did he forget the hermit. Every day he climbed the mountain, to give him his bowl of rice. And every day he found the hermit sitting quietly in front of his cave. He looked down over the forests and the lake. He saw the rich farms, and the quiet river curved about them like an arm. The lowing of the cattle, the cries of the herd boys came to his ears. But he never spoke again to Wang Li.

He had said what needed to be said. And being so wise, he said nothing more.

When he had finished the story, the Prince's voice behind the screen murmured sleepily, "What a pleasant evening!" And one of the courtiers silently escorted Cricket from the room.

That night, in his bed above the palace kitchens, he could scarcely sleep for wondering if the Prince were resting. In the morning he rejoiced with all the kingdom to hear that the royal child had slept for several hours and had awakened refreshed like a flower brightened by the dew.

It was with more courage, in the evening, that Cricket again bowed low to the chrysanthemum screen, and asked if he might be allowed to read the story of "The Scarlet Butterfly," for that was the name which appeared in characters, exquisite as the wings of flying swallows, along the right edge of the magic page when he drew it reverently from the breast of his gown.

"Read, and may the tale be as delightful as was the tale of Wang Li," said the Prince's voice.

So, amid the silent attention of the courtiers, Cricket bowed once more towards the screen and read.

THE SCARLET BUTTERFLY

Early one morning a band of soldiers passed through a poor fishing village. To the simple inhabitants they seemed terrible as dragons with the sunlight gleaming on the black scales of their armour and their faces scarcely human beneath their beetling helmets. Some were on horseback with two swords stuck through their girdles, and others trudged on foot, carrying tall pikes whose blades glittered to the rhythm of their marching. Behind these followed horses heavily laden with loot from some castle, and behind these came still other horses, and litters carrying the wounded.

It was the leader himself who halted for a moment at the door of a poor house at the outskirts of the village and called for its owners. They ran out, bowing almost to the ground, a middle-aged fisherman and his wife, who thought each moment might be their last.

"Take this child," said the warrior, pointing to a little girl held in the arms of a retainer. "Bring her up if you will, or drown her if you will." And he rode on without turning his head.

"We call her Scarlet Butterfly," the soldier said, lifting the child to the ground, and then he, too, rode on to join the others pouring steadily through the village like a river, surging up the hills through the pines, and at last disappearing forever from the sight of the fishermen.

But there, as witness that this had been no dream, all about them lay the marks of hoofs and feet in the dust of the road, and there was the child standing as she had been left, a little figure with blue-black hair cut to her shoulders opening and shutting like a fan when she moved, and dressed in only a scarlet undergarment.

The man and the woman to whom she had been given, took her into the house and fed her. She fell asleep over her rice.

"She is exhausted," they said. "She has ridden far."

All the village hummed that morning with talk. No net was dragged along the beaches, no boat put out to sea although the day was calm. Everyone crowded in and out of the cottage door, talking over the great happening that had taken place. The town was so out of the way, so few people ever came here

1298156

except the pearl merchants, that until now they had heard only rumours of the civil war in which two rival clans were locked in a death struggle. Who was this child? Why had she been spared? Across her right hand was a fresh cut, but there was no other mark on her.

"Mark my words," said her new foster mother, "she has been well brought up. Hungry as she was, she ate most honourably." And from the fine oval of her face and the beauty of her eyes, it was generally decided by the village that she was of noble parentage. She was too young to answer their questions, and soon they ceased to ask any. Who were they to interfere in the affairs of their superiors? He who puts his finger between the lobster's claws is sure to be pinched.

So Scarlet Butterfly grew up with the other village children, dressed like them and accustomed to what they were accustomed, but always different, at once more fiery and more gentle. With them she learned to swim in the shallow water and dig deep holes in the sand. Then when the fishermen dragged their great nets ashore, she ran with the others to watch the fish that gleamed among the weeds, and the curious sea monsters with claws or arms like spiders.

As she grew older, Scarlet Butterfly learned from

her foster mother the art of pearl-diving. For it was really on its pearls that the village lived, and it was the women who made the best divers, as they could stay under water longer than the men. It was a hard and dangerous life, but Scarlet Butterfly did not fear hardship and danger.

She loved the feeling of the cool water closing over her head as, with open eyes, she swam towards the floor of the ocean. Fish darted across her path like bright-coloured birds; the seaweeds of which she must beware seemed like forests in another country, and through them she could catch glimpses of white sand and coral towers. She could stay under water longer than any of the other girls, for her courage gave her endurance.

And when her work was done she loved to sit

on the rocks with her foster mother combing the tangled wave of her wet hair, and at last twisting it up before the mirror of a rock pool, while the older woman told her stories and the long afternoon shadows of the pine trees on the cliff fell across the seethe of foam along the shore.

When Scarlet Butterfly was nearly sixteen years old her foster father died and the two women were left alone. They had to work harder than ever to earn their living. There was less time for telling stories, and not so much rice in the pot. When night came the girl sank on her mats and slept without turning. But one night she had a dream. A beautiful woman, dressed in such fine robes as the village had never seen, appeared to her and bade her go to a certain cliff not far away, under which the water lay very deep. There she was to dive until she found a treasure of which she was not to speak until she was given a sign that the time had come.

Scarlet Butterfly awoke and, dressing quietly, crept out of the cottage without rousing her foster mother. It was a summer night and a full moon shone on the sea, whose ripples appeared like scales of a dragon encircling Japan. But where the moon was not reflected, the water was black and icy cold to her touch.

The Scarlet Butterfly

Had the dream been a true one? There was a sudden movement in the branches of the pine above her, which might be a demon or might be only a crane disturbed by her passing. The cliff was across the bay from the village and the road wound close to its edge. Looking back, she could see no light behind any of the paper windows of the houses. She thought that every human being in the world was asleep, but surely spirits were abroad! Still Scarlet Butterfly did not turn back.

With a prayer she entered into the dark water below the cliff. How could she see anything in those frozen depths? Yet without hesitation she followed her dream, swimming deeper and deeper towards the unseen floor of the sea. As she swam she saw a diffused light below her which at first she thought must be some reflection of the moon, but reaching towards it with her hand she found a flat solid object which she lifted and with some difficulty brought back to the surface.

Once safe on the beach, she saw in her hand a round steel mirror bright as the day it was first polished. The back was decorated with a design of flowers, and through a loop of metal hung a scarlet tassel. A mirror, she knew, was the symbol of a woman, just as a sword was of a man, and each was

regarded as sacred and handed down from parent to child. Full of wonder, Scarlet Butterfly leaned forward to see her reflection in its moon-shaped surface, but instead of her own face framed in her dark wet hair, she could see only what appeared to be the entrance of some daimyo's castle with guards standing about it.

Greatly surprised, she hurried home, where she hid her treasure, and creeping between the quilts fell asleep again, her wet hair trailing across the mats.

Not long after this occurrence another marvel befell, but this time it was no secret and all the village rejoiced at her good fortune. While diving she discovered an unusually large oyster and, upon opening it, found a pearl of perfect shape and great size.

Such a pearl had never been seen in the village, and all advised Scarlet Butterfly to make her way to the city which lay some forty or fifty miles distant, where she might hope to find a purchaser worthy of such a jewel. Accordingly she set forth alone, for her foster mother was too weak to walk so far. With her she secretly carried the mirror, and the pearl was in a small box hanging from her girdle. Her way led along the road at the edge of the cliff where she had dived, and as she walked she wondered if her mirror could have dropped from a pack-horse's saddle on that morning so long before when the soldiers had left her in the village.

But soon her thoughts turned to other matters. She had never before been far from home and now the farms and the rice terraces and the little boys flying their kites seemed far stranger than anything she had known in her world of fish and corals.

After several days she came to the outskirts of the city, but she never reached its markets, for just outside she saw a castle, and the very gate guarded by soldiers which had appeared on the bright surface of the mirror. Instantly she knew that the sign had come for her to speak, and going up to the soldiers, she begged to be taken to the lord of the castle.

The daimyo was seated on a cushion playing chess

when an attendant told him that a beautiful young girl from one of the fishing villages prayed for an interview with him.

"Let her be summoned," said the great lord, thinking that this was perhaps another complaint against his tax gatherers. And so Scarlet Butterfly was brought before him and, although she came in such mean attire, everyone was struck by her natural grace and air of breeding.

"To begin at the beginning, my lord," she said, "I had a dream." And when she had told him her dream, he asked:

"What was the appearance of this woman who came to you?"

"She was slender as a willow," answered Scarlet Butterfly, "and her lips were very red."

At hearing this, the face of the daimyo became quiet, as though he wished to hide his emotion, and he said, "Continue."

Then she told him of finding the mirror and of the reflection of his castle gate in it, and of the pearl which had brought her to the city.

"That is all I know, most honourable lord," she ended.

At his command she took the mirror from the little bundle she had with her and, bowing low, presented it to him, and he, taking it, said:

"This is the mirror of my wife, the Lady Dawn-Flower, who perished when my castle was burned." And he asked Scarlet Butterfly more questions. When had she come to the fishing village? How old had she been? What had she been wearing?

When she had answered all his questions, he said:

"It may be that you are my daughter, or it may be that you are an impostor and worthy of death. It is possible that you found the mirror and made up your story from common gossip. Do you know nothing more?"

The girl shook her head. "I know only what I have told you, my lord, but if you ask in my village they will tell you that Scarlet Butterfly never lies."

At her words joy came into the daimyo's eyes, but he only asked:

"Whence came that name?"

"The soldier who carried me on his saddle said that I was so called, my lord," Scarlet Butterfly answered.

Then the daimyo ordered a feast to be spread, and a room to be prepared for Scarlet Butterfly, and beautiful robes to be brought for her to wear, and a litter to be sent to bring back her foster mother to the castle.

"For now I am assured you are my daughter, and the rest of the tale is mine to tell," he said. And while the courtiers leaned forward, the great lord went on:

"Many years ago during the wars I was leading my retainers against the enemy far from here. My castle was left in charge of my young wife and a few Samurai, for we considered it impossible for the foe to slip past us. Nevertheless we were mistaken. A large band penetrated our province and laid siege to the castle. My wife, armed with her halbert, led the defence of the walls in a way worthy of the

44

blood she bore. She was killed with all our followers and the castle sacked and burned. When the news reached me I rode night and day. Smoke rose where I had last seen high roofs and only one living creature greeted me. It was the nurse who had been in charge of my little daughter. She was dying, but she told me first how the enemy had rushed into my child's apartments. My daughter, who was not yet five years old, faced them fearlessly and struck aside one of their swords with her hand.

"As the blood spread over her palm she looked at it and said, 'Look! the scarlet butterfly!'

"Then the leader, who had witnessed the scene, was amazed at her courage and ordered her life to be spared. This the nurse told me and me alone before she died. I had thought my child carried far to the south and never dared hope to see her again, but the spirit of her mother and her own courage have brought her back to me."

Scarlet Butterfly was weeping with happiness. Gently her father took her right hand in his and opened it. There along the palm was a deep thin scar. He held it up to his followers.

"Behold," he said in a voice full of pride. "Behold the branch upon which that butterfly alighted."

45

When the story was finished, the Prince behind the screen murmured as before, "What a pleasant evening!" And an attendant, finger on lip, led Cricket out.

The next day the court and nation rejoiced to hear that the royal child had slept more than ever before since his illness and that there seemed hope that the power of the story-telling page was driving the demon of sleeplessness from the imperial bed. And that evening when Cricket asked permission to read, the voice from behind the screen answered clearly and eagerly:

"What is the tale of the magic scroll to-night?"

And Cricket answered respectfully:

"Light of the Nation, it is 'The Horse of the War God.'"

"Read!" commanded the unseen Prince, and, amid the silent attention of the courtiers, Cricket bowed again towards the screen, and began.

THE HORSE OF THE WAR GOD

The boy liked best tending the white horse in his shrine near the temple. All day the beautiful animal stood looking out through the pine trees towards the lake beyond, drowsing sometimes, and sometimes rousing himself to stamp his hoofs and switch his long tail. Then he would whinny in a long note that clanged like a trumpet through the temple grove and out across the roofs of the village, so that the villagers said, "The horse of the War God is calling to his master."

But when the boy came to the shrine with food and water for the white horse, and cloths to clean his glossy sides and combs to unravel the cascades of his mane and tail, the horse arched his neck down to his shoulder, and breathed softly against his face. No one except the horse loved the boy who was an orphan and a temple servant, and no one but the boy really loved the horse, though the villagers on their way to the temple of the War God stopped at his shrine to admire him and make their offerings.

And in fact so beautiful a steed could not be found in the length and breadth of the countryside. He was as white as the snow-covered crest of Fuji-yama; his neck was as curved as a warrior's bow; and he was without blemish. If the God of War ever wished a worthy mount when he should ride out to meet the enemy, this was the animal.

But being a horse in a shrine is monotonous. It needed fortitude to endure the long hours when the rain drummed ceaselessly on the roof or the snow swept past the heavy open lattice of his dwelling. Then the boy would come slipping away from his other duties to bring his friend some special treat to make the day go quickly for them both.

He was a plain-looking boy, used to bearing heat and cold, used to harsh words and sometimes blows, used to wet garments and the feel of snow about his bare ankles. Since he had served the temple the priests had not been unkind to him. But to tell the truth they were a lazy lot, and more work fell on his shoulders than they were meant to bear. The head priest was an old man not fitted to serve the God of War. All his thoughts were on his garden and the etiquette of the tea ceremony. He never noticed that the tiles were beginning to fall from the temple roof like leaves from an old tree, nor

48

that fewer and fewer of the villagers came to so run-down a temple. The other priests were shiftless and as long as their bowls were full of rice each day they did not care how the rats might carry away the offerings set on the tables before the god. Only the white horse in his separate shrine shone like a jewel in its case under the untiring care of the boy.

One day an elderly man came to the temple. For many years he had been away from his village. Now when he saw what had happened to the temple he was indignant. He had to speak out his mind to someone and as the boy happened to be the only one near, it was to him he spoke.

"This is a lamentable state of affairs indeed," he exclaimed. "When I was a young man this place was one of the most beautiful in Japan. People came from distant provinces to worship at the spot where the dragon died."

"What dragon, sir, may I venture to inquire?" asked the boy.

"Are you a temple servant and do not even know about the dragon?" cried the man. "Every village child used to know the story. Long ago on the bare mountain slope above this temple there lived a dragon which laid waste the countryside. Hero after hero went to fight with the monster but each left

49

his bones to whiten the entrance of the dragon's cave. At last a young nobleman at the Emperor's court determined to take upon himself the quest. He was only sixteen years old, but he had a will like a sword, and would listen to no attempts to dissuade him. So, all in armour, he rode away towards this abode of death.

"But he was not alone. With him came a young girl, a lady-in-waiting at the court, who loved him, and insisted on sharing with him the dangers of the encounter. Surely now," said the villager, breaking off, "you remember the rest of the story?"

"No, honoured sir," said the boy, "I have never heard it before."

"Shame be to this temple and its priests, then!" said the old man. "When the young nobleman came near the entrance of the cave, he left the maiden with the horses in this grove of trees, while he went up to face the monster in its lair. Signs enough and to spare he found of its presence, but the dragon had retreated to the depths of its cave. No taunts could induce it to come forth, for it knew that in this boy's hand lay its appointed death.

"Now dragons are very fond of music, and when the girl heard her beloved in vain summoning the creature to battle, she remembered a flute she had

brought with her to solace her companion on the way. So, drawing this from its case, she placed it to her lips. Although her heart was nearly bursting with terror she played on it so beautifully that the dragon forgot its forebodings and came out of the cavern to hear, and so fell before the young warrior's sword.

"But when the boy leaped down the hillside shouting out the news of his victory, he found all silent among the trees. His love was lying on the ground, her flute still in her hand. The struggle between her great courage and her great fear had been more than her slight body could bear, and with the last note of music, she had died. This temple was built to the God of War to commemorate the killing of the dragon. Oh, shame that this story should be told here as something strange and out-of-the-way!" And shaking his head the old man returned to the village.

Perhaps until then the boy had taken for granted the way things went at the temple. But now he saw everything with new eyes. Here a great deed had been enacted long ago and honoured in the building of these shrines. How wrong of the priests of to-day to allow the place to fall into disrepute! In a few years no one would come any more; the temple would be empty and ruined. Only the pine trees and the rocks of the steep mountainside would remember the young warrior's courage; only the wind would tell of the song the maiden had played.

Going about his tasks, the boy brooded over these things. He determined to speak to the head priest if he had the opportunity, and only a few days later the chance came. He had been ordered to clean out the pool which was overlooked by the small building where the priest invited his guests for tea. Fastening his garments high, the boy waded into the cold water with a broom of twigs, sweeping the rocks and hollows clean of the gathered silt. When all was shining he looked at his work, not quite satisfied. At last he broke off a branch of scarlet maple leaves—for it was autumn—and let it catch between two boulders.

"I see that in spite of your rough exterior you have **the soul of an artist**," said a voice behind him,

and he turned to find that the head priest was standing near. "I suppose you are one of the temple servants? I think I have noticed you."

"The horse of the honourable War God is my especial charge," murmured the boy, bowing.

"You have shown a real sense of art in sweeping the pool," said the head priest.

This was the time to speak. Confused by his own daring, he said, almost in a whisper, "Pray forgive me. The temple, your honour must have noticed—the tiles! Ever since my insignificant arrival—how few people come! Matters grow worse and worse! So few offerings!"

But the head priest stopped him, raising one old hand.

"These matters disturb the tranquillity of my thoughts. I must suggest to you that you have behaved unsuitably in speaking to me in this manner." And without again glancing at the boy he disappeared within the shadows of the temple.

"Alas!" thought the other, gazing after him, "he is so old and gentle, he scarcely sees the world he lives in and cannot rouse himself to save us." And he took his disappointment to the shrine of the white horse.

A few nights later there arose a great storm. From behind the hill above the temple it poured. And with the wind came great torrents of rain that fell from the sky like cataracts, lit by flares of lightning, and resounding with thunder.

Restless was the sleep of the priests that night and no one dared so much as to open a door upon the mad world outside, except the boy, who slipped away and ran through the turmoil to join the white horse.

"I could not leave you alone," he whispered, "when all the demons of the storm are loose."

But the horse did not seem frightened. He nuzzled the boy's face, and then stood quietly, until at last the boy fell asleep, wet and cold as he was. But no sooner was he asleep than he heard a great voice calling:

"Come hither, horse! Come hither that I may ride!"

And looking up, he saw the white horse standing above him with raised head. The shrine doors had opened of themselves and outside he saw standing the dark form of the God of War himself, all in armour, the red lacquer of his face gleaming terribly in the flashes of lightning.

Then the boy prostrated himself, but above him he heard the white horse answer:

"And where shall we ride, O my master?"

And the God of War answered in a voice that mingled with the thunder above the sound of the increasing cataract of the rain:

"Against this temple of mine which has dishonoured me, shall we ride! And against this village which has forgotten me, shall we ride! And not one

wall of this unworthy temple shall stand in the dawn, and not one man shall open his eyes upon the morning's sun!"

Then said the white horse:

"Shall no one be spared, O my master?"

And the War God cried:

"Not one shall be spared."

Then said the white horse:

"I will not come."

And at his words a silence seemed to come upon the tempest, a suspense that was broken only by the groaning of the trees.

Then the War God cried in a voice that shook the shrine:

"I will lash you with lightning! You shall feel the weight of my wrath like fire upon you! Once more I command you! Come forth!"

And the boy felt the horse trembling above him, but once more he said:

"I will not come, O my master."

Then the boy heard the rattle of the War God's armour, as he moved his arm, and he shrank waiting for what was to come. But instead of the consuming flame he expected, one more question pierced the storm:

"Why do you defy me?"

And the white horse answered:

"O my master, I defy you for the sake of love. There is one here who has served me since first we met, putting my need always before his own. It is for his sake that I have presumed to disobey you, and for his sake I yield up the life I have forfeited."

The night grew heavy with consideration, but at last the voice of the War God came:

"Obedience is a virtue. Gratitude is also a virtue. For this one time I will not demand that you choose between them. And for your sake I will spare this temple and this village, though I shall return unless they mend their ways, and as a proof I leave my mark upon their door."

And with that came a last crash and blaze of thunder and lightning outside, and afterwards the storm died away, and even the wind was silent and only the heavy rain-drops dripping from the trees remained to show what a flood had poured over them.

Then having embraced the knees of the white horse, the boy ran through the darkness and roused the priests, whom he found huddled together. He told them what he had seen and heard, and some were filled with awe and some scoffed and said he had been dreaming. But at dawn they found that the door of the temple itself had been struck by lightning, and the marvel was that there remained upon it a white scar shaped exactly like an arrow.

And seeing this, no one doubted the boy's story any longer. The old head priest resigned his office and retired into a life of contemplation, and the other priests set about repairing the temple they had so long neglected, and through all Japan the story spread until pilgrimages were made from the furthest provinces to behold the wonderful white horse who had turned the War God from his purpose, and the arrow-shaped mark of the lightning upon the temple door.

So between the offerings made by the pilgrims and the busy lives of the priests, the temple became more beautiful than it had ever been. In time the boy rose to be head priest, governing the affairs of the temple prudently and humbly, and never forgetting the love that bound him to the white horse, with whom he still spent long hours that made the days pass happily for them both.

"That is a very delightful story," said the Prince. "Last night I slept long and well, and I am assured that it is your tales which are driving away the horrid demon of sleeplessness." Then he ordered fine robes of silk to be given to Cricket.

When Cricket went again to the Prince's apartments the attendants whispered to each other that in his splendid new robes he had a very fine air. He could scarcely believe that three or four days ago he had been running errands for his harsh master and sleeping in a garret. He wondered if the silk merchant had heard of all that had befallen him, and if he were angry to find his apprentice gone. He knew that his mother in their little village could know nothing of his adventures, but he yearned to go to her and ask her if he had done as she would have wished. With a heart full of wonder at the strange life he had led ever since he had picked up the loose page beside the burned house, he begged permission to read "The Pavilion of the Birds," since that was the title he found written in characters as lovely as grasses, some upright and some bent and broken by the wind.

And when the permission was granted, Cricket, amid the silent attention of the courtiers, bowed once more towards the screen, and read.

THE PAVILION OF THE BIRDS

There was once an old Chinese gentleman who desired tranquillity more than anything else in the world. But that was the one thing he could not have. He had riches and a beautiful old house, and a grove of trees shading it with their green parasols in summer and in the winter delighting him with their beautiful branches which sometimes seemed to be covered with blossoms of snow.

He had a moon terrace with seats of green porcelain from which to watch the moon when it rose like a great pearl among the twisting cloud dragons.

He had a garden whose wall was pierced by openings cut in the shapes of fruits and flowers. There the wind never ruffled his pond, or cooled his tea when he sat in his pavilion listening to the faint, faint clash of wind bells.

But tranquillity he did not have. If he sat down by a latticed window when the sun of the early spring lay like a cool hand on his heart, he was sure to hear the sound of ears being boxed, and a woman's voice screaming:

"You little monster! How dare you look out of the door when you should be sweeping? You're not worth the rice we feed you on!"

Or if the old gentleman in the evening sat playing the harp to himself, he was certain to be interrupted by someone bursting energetically into his room with a clop, clop, clopping of shoes to ask if there was anything he needed.

And if he sat on the moon terrace watching the stars in the sky like seeds close-set in a dark flower, a servant was sure to appear, bowing and saying:

"Excuse me, sir, but the honourable mistress fears that you will catch cold "

So with one thing and another the old gentleman had everything but peace. It was his niece who was the cause of all his woe. She was a widow, and since she had come to live with him as a housekeeper, everything had gone wrong.

And what a housekeeper she was! She was always interrupting the servants at their work, telling the gardeners to do the wrong thing, and taking care of the old gentleman just when he most wanted to be left alone.

His food was always cold by the time it reached him because she had stopped the maid in the passage to change the seasoning. She told so many people to mend his clothes that no one ever did it; and she was so stingy that she put water in his wines until his friends no longer enjoyed coming to the house. Altogether she made him miserable with the best intentions in the world. And the old gentleman was so kind-hearted that he could not bear to tell her to go.

But one day his patience gave way. He was sitting in a place where he hoped she would not find him, having slyly told a servant that he might walk among the trees. Over his head the first bees were buzzing among the blossoms and the old man in his padded silk coat was enjoying the warmth and planning a poem in his mind, when suddenly he heard the hated click, click of jade ornaments, and there was his niece.

"Come! Come! my august uncle! Is it wise at your age to sit here with your feet on the damp marble? I beg you, take your honoured way into the house again."

The old gentleman stared at his niece, and she looked solid like a rock that was about to roll on him and crush him.

"Even the aged chrysanthemum shines brighter for the dew," he said, and then he added with sudden determination, "You are still a young woman. Why do you not seek another husband? Your dowry would be no mean one."

"I am unworthy of your thoughts," cried the niece, her face turning white at the idea of leaving all her power in this great house. "You know, most learned uncle, that Confucius advises widows against marrying again." And two tears rolled out of her little eyes and ran down her fat cheeks.

"I beg you, do not weep," said the old gentleman, immediately filled with pity, and his niece hid her face behind her embroidered sleeves so that he should not see her satisfied smile.

What a kind heart he had! Better that he should live in misery than cause pain, he thought. But he felt suddenly tired. He no longer cared about the spring sunshine nor the bees nor his poem.

"I am sleepy," he said. "I shall go in and rest." And so he left her.

But when he had lain on his bed for a few minutes he felt refreshed, and a desire for the sunlight and the budding trees fell upon him. He rose, put on his padded coat and his silk cap again, and crept outdoors. No, there was no sight nor sound of his niece. He walked through his grounds and as he walked he took a delight in the trees that arched over his head. There was his gate and there the road he knew so well.

He walked rapidly for a few minutes and then he saw coming to meet him some men who seemed to be the servants of some great man. They saluted him, bowing low and calling him by name, and said that their master, having heard of his renown as a scholar, begged the honour of a visit, as his house was near at hand.

"Very willingly," said the old gentleman, wondering, however, who this important neighbour could be of whom he had never heard. But his surprise was much greater when in a few minutes they came to an elaborate gate and saw before them a palace, with court opening upon court and garden upon garden and mansion rising behind mansion. The walls were all painted a beautiful green like the finest jade and the tiles were of brightest blue. Young men and women in gauzy garments moved about here and there, and from a pavilion came the sound of a harp. Over the door he read:

The Mansion of Green Delight

The old gentleman was escorted into a hall hung with curtains embroidered with birds and flowers. At the end of the room between a double row of pillars rose a throne and on it was seated a man of benign and princely bearing surrounded by a circle of attendants. When he saw the newcomer he rose to his feet to meet him.

"Welcome," he cried, "your fame as a scholar has preceded you. I beg you to sit with me and as we sip our wine let us talk together of the matters which interest us."

Servants quickly brought jade cups filled with wine, and fruit heaped up in dishes. The Prince pledged the old man who was somewhat bewildered but determined to enjoy this chance escape from the dreary afternoons shared with his niece. After a few minutes the Prince said, "May I suggest, sir, that we play the game of poetry together? Here is my first line:

"And now the icicles have turned to tasselled chains——"

Then he stopped and looked expectantly at the old gentleman who immediately added:

"And golden birds sing through the spring-time rains."

"That is charming," said the Prince. "Nor was there time for one to draw so much as a breath before you had capped my verse. Curiously enough you gave the name of my daughter who is called Golden Bird because of her sweet voice. Since you happened to invoke her, she must join us." And he sent attendants to call the Princess.

In a few minutes she came, and the old gentleman thought he had never seen anyone so delightful. Her hair was coiled like a cloud and decked with flowers. Over an undergarment of embroidered green she wore a gauze cloak of yellow. He had never seen anything so small as her feet, both of which he might have held on one palm, and her talk was as graceful as her appearance.

But suddenly in the middle of their enjoyment, cries were heard outside, and a crowd of servants burst into the room, all babbling with fear.

The Prince tried to calm them.

"What is the trouble, my friends?" he demanded.

"They are attacking us——"

"Save yourself, my lord!"

"The foundations are tottering——"

Some ran this way and that, some cowered in the corners of the hall, a few hurried to arms and rolled the war drums. From outside might be heard a steady and ominous boom, jarring the whole building as though some enemy were battering at the doors with rams. The Princess ran to the old gentleman and caught his arm.

"Pray give us shelter!" she cried. "We cannot defend ourselves!"

The old gentleman murmured, "If you will deign——"

But she broke in, "Why talk of deigning when we may be killed at any moment?"

With that the old man was stirred to action. He helped Golden Bird hurry down the stairs into the gardens at the rear of the palace, followed by her father and all the court. Somehow they found the road, and in haste made their way to his own house. With Golden Bird on his arm he turned to welcome the others, and turning, he awoke.

It had been a dream. He had been lying all this time on his own bed in his own room. But what was that? There, perched on his breast was a beautiful little bird looking down into his face. And outside he heard a thousand birds twittering and singing among his trees.

Saying nothing to anyone, he arose and put on his padded silk coat as he had done in his dream and followed the path of his dream to the road, which in the afternoon sunlight seemed marked with many foot-prints turning in at his gate. The little bird went with him, sometimes perching on his shoulder and sometimes flying about him, darting here and there, twittering a sweet and melancholy note. Some distance up the road, they came to a fine grove of trees where a dozen woodcutters had recently begun to work. The trees were groaning under the blows of the axes, their green crests shivering and swaying as the men bent their backs to the task. Far up among the new leaves of the branches the old gentleman could see dozens of nests, deserted save for a few excited birds that flew about with despairing screams.

The little bird crept into the breast of his coat as though to hide her eyes from the sight, and suddenly the old man knew for certain what wonderful thing had befallen him. In a vision of sleep he had conversed with the Prince of the Birds and visited his palaces. The attack had been that of the woodcutters; it was his hosts of a few hours ago who were now flying about in his own grove, and it was

Princess Golden Bird herself who rested against his heart.

"If I could only save your kingdom!" he murmured, "but I cannot. Only in my own grove can I promise a safe refuge."

His niece noticed nothing.

"What a lot of birds there are this year," she said that evening. "I see you have found one, honourable uncle. I suppose it hurt its wing. Look out, it might peck you."

The old gentleman said nothing, but he found a hairpin ornament that had once belonged to his dead wife and fastened it above his desk near the south window. There sat the little bird by day when she was not upon his shoulder. While he was writing or studying she would be silent, but when he gazed at the green world outside, she would burst into the loveliest of songs until his heart sang to hear her. But best of all, when the household was asleep, she turned again into the Princess. While the niece snored after a day of interfering with everyone, the old gentleman and the Princess wandered out to the moon terrace, where together they watched the moon rise like a pearl among the dragons of the clouds, and she never told him that he was old and must not enjoy anything.

"See, there is the Spinning Damsel," the old man would say, pointing to one bright star, "and there the silver river in the sky separates her from her love, the Herd Boy."

"But they will meet yet," the Princess would answer. "The magpies make a bridge for her once a year, and on it she walks safely to her husband."

"I am glad of that," the old scholar would say, thinking of his dead wife whom he had loved. But now all his thoughts were happy ones, with the Princess for company. What songs she sang to him, just brushing the harp strings with her finger tips! How neatly she mended his clothes, while he read aloud to her and the brazier sent forth a sleepy fragrance of incense. How she clapped her hands together in wonder over the beauty of his poems!

> *"Like a spring wind that passes*
> *She goes by.*
> *Like wind bells sound her ornaments of jade.*
> *Her path you trace in flowers, and my heart*
> *Counts all my hours as garlands she has made."*

That was one of the poems the old gentleman wrote to thank Golden Bird for the happiness she brought him. She received it humbly. She felt it an honour to serve so kind a man and so distinguished a scholar.

But perhaps her greatest service was of another sort. One day the niece appeared, looking agitated.

"I have been thinking over your advice, honourable uncle," she said, "and I have decided that, as always, you know best. I should be willing to sacrifice my life again to a husband if the go-between can find a suitable match—though what you'll do without me I can't guess. I've worn myself to the bone in your service."

Then she paused and suddenly cried out in a frightened way:

"Every night I have the most terrible dream of birds pecking at me with their beaks and beating me with their wings. I will not stay under this roof."

And before the gentle old man could find an answer, she had flounced out of the room and the bird on its jewelled perch was singing, singing a song that filled the old man's heart with tranquil gaiety.

That night the Prince slept long and well, and all the nation rejoiced at the news.

The next evening the Prince greeted Cricket cheerfully from behind the screen, and the courtiers had a cheerful look, and there were more lights in the room shining upon the panels painted with scenes from the lives of warriors and heroes.

"May you live a thousand years!" exclaimed Cricket, and when he had asked and received permission to read the story whose title he found written in characters as clear and angular as the legs and wing-cases of beetles, amid the silent attention of the courtiers, he bowed once more towards the screen and read "The Deer Boy."

THE DEER BOY

The mother deer had recently lost her fawn and when she heard the cry near the cave mouth she stopped, stretching out her long neck, while her eyes shone with wonder. The child saw her; perhaps he even smelled the milk that pressed against her udders. At all events he rose to his feet and made towards her. He was too young to walk very steadily and once he tripped and fell, startling the deer into sudden flight. But at his wail the creature hesitated and circled back, sniffing the wind. She was afraid of the human smell, but something told her that this was a baby-thing come to take the place of her lost fawn. Bit by bit the child drew nearer and at last the deer let him touch her and drink her warm milk. Little she knew of the lady, dressed in rough peasant's clothes but with a face like a flower, who lay dead in the cave, too exhausted with hardships and overwhelmed with disasters to live on. Little the deer knew of the civil wars of the great clans of Japan. She only knew that she felt every day more and more tender towards this small thing that was so helpless and followed her about on such unsteady feet. Since he could not yet bound away at her side at the hint of danger, she taught him to hide in the underbrush and lie still until all was safe and she could return to him. Later she brought him to the herd, which at first stamped and snorted at so strange a presence, but soon accepted him as one of the fawns and thought no more about it.

As he grew older, it was a lovely sight to see the child running at his foster mother's side, swift as any of the deer about him. He, too, could scent a breeze and know when the taint of danger came near. His eyes could make out the slightest movement, his ears could hear the slightest sound. Of course he knew no words but he could make himself understood by the deer, though sometimes he would surprise them by uttering a human laugh. At such times they would look at him and shake their horns, but the Deer Boy would only laugh again.

The herd roamed among the high moors under the mountain tops, far from the villages. The white fogs flowed about them; the great red dawns shone on their dew-wet coats until they gleamed like copper inlaid with spots of pale gold, and their browsing heads were outlined against the moon. Wherever

they went the Deer Boy went too, growing thin in the winter with the rest of the herd, and waxing fat in the summer.

He must have been twelve years old before he saw his first man. There was a rough road leading across the moors with a stone statue of the god Gizo beside it, on whose shoulders the crows loved to sit. It was a long and dangerous way, and was little used.

But one day the Deer Boy was wandering alone. He found the path and followed it carefully, listening and watching and smelling the breeze for a hint of danger. He found the Gizo and stared at it. This was not a deer, no, he was sure of that. But it was familiar. It stood on feet as he stood, it had a face something like that which he had glimpsed in the moorland pools and known for his own. But it had only the smell of rock, it made no sound, it did not move. He touched it and it was hard. He was so intent that for once he forgot to be careful, and the pedlar was near at hand before he was aware of him. The Deer Boy stared for a fraction of an instant straight into the stranger's face, and then leaped away, running with the speed of a bird's shadow.

But the pedlar had seen enough. He told his story to the villagers and then people who had gathered brushwood on the mountains remembered that they had seen foot-prints of a naked human foot among the pronged tracks of the deer at the muddy margins of pools. Everyone longed to see the Deer Boy with their own eyes. Was he a mountain spirit who ruled the deer? Or was he a deer that could bewitch itself into human form like the foxes, and come as a stranger into the villages?

People discussed it around the braziers in the evenings. Some even took offerings of food and left them on the moor for the Deer Boy in case he was a god, but though he came near and touched them when the people were gone, he never tasted a morsel.

For several years the fame of the Deer Boy grew, until at last it reached the ears of the Emperor himself.

It happened to be the springtime when the

Emperor was wearied of court functions and longed to be again in the saddle.

"Let us by all means go and see this Deer Boy," he exclaimed. "I feel it is very important. The Prime Minister shall attend to affairs of state while we are gone."

Great preparations were made: horses were groomed, tents and cooking utensils were overhauled, and hunters and beaters gathered for the royal hunting party. The villagers were somewhat aghast to find that their mountain spirit was to be hunted like a fox, but the Emperor of course could do no wrong.

At dawn one bright morning the trackers went out. When their experienced eyes had located where the herd was feeding and had made out the prints of the Deer Boy's feet, they sent for His Imperial Highness. He came riding among his courtiers, merry with the spring lightness of the air. The hunters, meanwhile, were forming a great loop about the deer. When suddenly the leader of the herd raised his antlered head and realized the danger, it was too late. From every direction at once the hunters burst into a shrill yelping and beat upon their gongs until the deer were in a panic. Then the Emperor rode up, and the hunters rushed in, and overpowering the Deer Boy, tied his wrists behind his back and dragged him before the ruler.

Some of the villagers who had followed the expedition expected to see him change into a deer and make off with the others, but there he stood, like any human boy, bound and helpless. And though he looked beautiful as a young god, he had no godlike speech with which to reprove the Emperor who was looking down at him with much interest from his saddle.

"I pray you ask this unworthy naked person where he comes from," he said to one of his courtiers.

But though the courtier asked the Deer Boy a dozen times, the Deer Boy made no answer.

"But it is the Emperor himself who deigns to inquire," cried the courtier in despair.

Still the Deer Boy only looked at them curiously, understanding nothing.

"I have been observing," the Emperor remarked, "and my observation is this. It appears to my penetration that this curious naked person does not understand our speech."

"Ah, he does not understand!" the courtiers exclaimed, surprised.

"It further appears to my penetration," went on the Emperor, "that he is not deaf."

"He is not deaf!" exclaimed the courtiers.

"Coming as we do from the capital we are much too wise to believe him a spirit like these ignorant villagers," continued the Emperor.

"Much too wise," murmured the courtiers.

"Besides that, he does not act like a spirit. A spirit would have turned into a deer or left us in a cold mist."

"Certainly that is the way of spirits," agreed the courtiers.

"So it is clear to my penetration that this is what I called him at the first, an unworthy naked person," summed up the Emperor with satisfaction.

"I have decided to have him brought back to the capital and given the training suitable to a human being," he went on, "but if he is to have the honour of accompanying us he must first be clothed. Here," said the Emperor to one of the hunters, "give him your robes."

But when they had unbound the Deer Boy's hands and put the hunter's clothes on him and rough sandals on his feet, he pulled them off and disdainfully tore them to shreds.

The Emperor turned to one of the courtiers

and ordered that his clothes be given to the Deer Boy.

And when the Deer Boy stood dressed in the garments of a gentleman all were surprised at his fine appearance, but he again pulled the clothes from him and would not wear them, although this time he did not tear them.

Then said the Emperor to the chief courtier, "Retire, I pray you, and let your robes be given to this unworthy naked person here."

And when they had put on the Deer Boy the robes of the chief courtier he looked like a prince. No one had ever seen a nobler figure. And at the touch of the soft rich silks an old memory stirred in the Deer Boy's mind, and he did not attempt to take off these new garments, but stood so proud and so at ease that everyone exclaimed.

"Surely this is the son of well-born parents," cried the Emperor. "He disdains the clothes of common people, but he is as much at one with courtly garments as a carp is with his scales."

"If it please your Shining Splendour," said one of the archers, "on the shoulder of this person while I was robing him I discerned the tattooing of a sun with its rays."

At that the Emperor covered his face with his hands and wept. Then he dismounted and embraced the Deer Boy.

"Surely," said the Emperor, "this is my nephew, son of his Royal Highness, my Younger Brother. When the dark armies of traitors dared fling their impious attack against the sacred throne many years ago, I led the armies of the south while his Royal Highness, my Younger Brother, led the armies of the north. The times were troubled and when we bade each other farewell we did so with the look of men who might not meet again. 'If I die,' said his Royal Highness, my Younger Brother, 'remember my wife and my little son whom I take with me. It may be that they will escape. Before I go to battle I shall mark him with the crest of the rising sun so that you may know him.' To me and to no one else his Royal Highness, my Younger Brother, spoke of

88

this sign. Months later word was brought of his death, but when at last I had conquered the traitors and moved gloriously northward, I could find no trace of her Royal Highness, my Younger Sister, or of this child. But behold even the deer of the mountains have recognized the sacredness of the royal blood and respectfully preserved this precious life until the appointed time."

And with that the Deer Boy was mounted on a splendid horse which he rode as though born to the saddle, and escorted back to the capital amid great rejoicings. There he learned to speak and write, to handle a sword, and to conduct himself gracefully at court functions, until there was scarcely his equal in the empire.

And the service of the deer was not forgotten. An imperial edict forbade the killing of any of the herd on pain of death, and undisturbed they roamed the high moors by day, and undisturbed by night lay at their ease watching the moon-whitened mists creep over the villages in the valleys below them.

But the Deer Boy never again ran at their sides nor gazed in wonder at the wayside Gizo.

When Cricket had finished his story, the Prince clapped his hands with pleasure.

"Let him be given a horse!" he cried. "Oh! oh! it is a good thing to feel sleepy!"

And the next day the news was publicly announced that the heir to the throne had slept all night long and would walk in the royal gardens. Cricket did not see him even at a distance, for he was busy in the imperial stables choosing a horse for himself from among six hundred of the beautiful creatures.

That evening when Cricket appeared, the Prince ordered the chrysanthemum screen removed, and for the first time the apprentice sat in the actual presence of such splendour, although he was much too respectful even to raise his eyes to the Prince's face. And one again a new title appeared on the magic page in characters clear and etched as the prints of sea-birds' feet on the wet sand, and when the Prince had granted permission, Cricket amid the silent attention of the courtiers, bowing low once more towards the spot where the Prince was sitting, read.

THE SPIRIT OF THE CAMELLIA

"Sweep the house so that not so much as a grain of rice sticks to the mats! If you don't hurry up with your work, you shall have no dinner, you bad child!"

The little girl bowed her head.

"The broom is so old! If you will give me a new one, I am sure I can do better," she said softly.

"A new one, indeed!" cried the woman. "I suppose that it's the broom that doesn't get the work done! Let's hear no more about it!"

Spring Breeze, for that was the little girl's name, dried her eyes, and went back to work. The broom was so old that she had to sweep and sweep in the same spot before it was clean. You would never have guessed to see her that she was a rich man's daughter. Her clothes were of faded cotton. Her clothes were patched. They were too small for her. Her hands were rough with the work they did. But in spite of her clothes she was very pretty, with a mouth ready to smile, and bright eyes.

She was much prettier indeed than fat Peony, her half-sister who sat near her on a low chair. Peony was sewing now and then on a piece of silk. But most of the time she was eating rice cakes from the dish beside her. She was dressed in fine clothes. In her hair were pretty ornaments. She had a cheerful greedy look, and was as kind as a greedy child can be.

When her mother had gone out of the room she said to Spring Breeze, "Our father will be home soon. Then you will not have to work so hard. Mother does not let him see how badly she treats you."

"How glad I shall be to see Father," said Spring Breeze.

"And he will bring us presents from the city!" went on Peony.

Spring Breeze went back to her sweeping. Even hard at work she looked like her name. There was something sweet and cool and fresh about her. As

94

she walked she swayed a little, like a young willow tree in a wind.

She could not help looking at Peony's rice cakes. It was so long since she had eaten a rice cake! Peony saw her glance and looked at the plate herself. There were only two cakes left. Should she give Spring Breeze one? She wanted to, but oh she wanted them so badly herself!

"I'd like to give you a cake, Spring Breeze," she said, helping herself, "but mother would be angry if I did."

It was just as well that she had eaten them herself, for just then her mother came back.

"I heard you talking!" she cried to Spring Breeze. "You can't talk and work too. Will you never try to please me?"

All day the little girls waited for the coming of their father. In the afternoon, Spring Breeze was told to wash herself and put on her silk dress. It, too, was rather faded. Not like Peony's new dress at all. And she had no pretty things to put in her hair like Peony. But there was a big camellia bush by the pool in the garden which she dearly loved. Spring Breeze picked one of its flowers, and put that in her hair.

She looked so lovely that even Peony's mother noticed it.

"Take that flower out of your hair!" she cried. "You are always trying to call attention to yourself."

So Spring Breeze sadly took the pink camellia flower out of her hair.

"I am so sorry," she said to the flower in a low voice. "Forgive me."

At that moment their father rode through the gate. His horse was a bay and its saddle and bridle were bright green. He looked very handsome, the little girls thought as they ran to meet him.

"Welcome, Father! Welcome!" they cried. And his wife cried, "Welcome! Welcome!"

She was smiling now. You would never have guessed that she was the same woman who was often so cross with Spring Breeze.

Now came the time for presents. There was a string of carved coral beads for Peony's mother. For the little girls there were two paper lanterns shaped like birds.

"Have you been good children while I was away?" their father asked.

"Peony is always good," said her mother, "but I can't say as much for Spring Breeze."

"I am sorry to hear that," said her father. "To obey is her duty. I am sure she will try harder."

Suddenly Peony gave a loud cry.

"Oh dear! Oh dear! I sat on my beautiful lantern and broke it," she sobbed.

"Never mind, dear," said her mother. "You shall have Spring Breeze's."

Poor Spring Breeze! When she could, she tiptoed away to the garden. There in the centre stood the great camellia bush beside the pool. Spring Breeze crept under the low branches. Inside was a little green room, where no one could see her. There she could cry.

But this afternoon she soon wiped away her tears. Something made her look through the low branches. And there on the marble bridge which crossed the pool stood a lady. She was very beautiful. Her dress was long and flowing and rose-coloured. It was

98

embroidered in green. The ornaments in her hair were of gold in the shape of butterflies. And she held a round fan in one beautiful hand.

"Why are you so sad, Spring Breeze?" she asked the little girl. "I have come to take you to a party."

At the end of the garden someone was singing. It was a lady dressed in white. Nearby sat old men with long beards smiling and drinking tea. Young men in the tall black hats of scholars talked together. Beautiful girls in bright clothes, and children played and laughed. Boys went about with great dishes of cakes and sweets. Now Spring Breeze could eat all the rice cakes she wanted! Everyone was glad to see her and seemed to know her. Everyone called her by name.

"What a beautiful summer we have had!" said one lady. "In the morning such dew! I wake up smiling. In the evening such fireflies! I myself prefer them to stars."

Just then Spring Breeze heard the angry voice of Peony's mother calling her. So she bowed low and with many thanks to everyone and especially to the lady in the rose-coloured dress, she ran away to the house.

Once she looked back, but she could see no one. They seemed all to have disappeared.

How Peony's mother scolded her!

"There are crumbs on your dress! You bad girl! You have been stealing food from the kitchen!" she shouted.

But from that day Spring Breeze lived two lives. In the house when her father was not there, she was scolded and made to work. Her share was the worst of everything. But in the garden she was happy. When she crept under the camellia bush there was never anyone to be seen. But when she looked out through its branches, there was the lady on the bridge, waiting.

What happy hours they passed together! Sometimes they wandered through the pines. The birds and little animals were not afraid of them. The birds lighted on Spring Breeze's shoulders. The little animals crowded about her feet. When it rained, a beautiful summer house appeared beside the pool. There Spring Breeze and the lady sat, hearing the rain on the tiles over their heads. It sounded like the swish of heavy silk. The lady taught Spring Breeze many things. The little girl learned to play on the harp and to sing old songs. She learned the slow stately court dances. She could recite poems, some happy, some sad. She learned to write poems of her own, and to paint with ink on a scroll of silk.

The Spirit of the Camellia

Few girls in all China were so gifted as Spring Breeze. But she was never proud. She only thought of pleasing the lady who was her friend. A strange thing was that her visits in the garden seemed to last for hours and hours, but when she returned to the house, she found that she had been gone for only a few minutes. No one had even noticed that she had been away.

So the days went by and the months, and the years, and now Spring Breeze and Peony were grown up. And one day word came that the Emperor in his far away palace wished to choose a wife for his eldest son.

North, south, east and west the court officials went, searching for beautiful young girls from whom the bride would be chosen. At last the official came to the house where Spring Breeze and Peony lived, and the girls were sent for.

As usual, Peony had been dressed in her best, her hair thick with ornaments. As usual, Spring Breeze wore an old gown, almost outgrown.

The elderly official looked at them both kindly.

"This maiden," he said, bowing to Spring Breeze, "shall return with me to the court. There with four hundred and ninety-nine other beautiful young girls she will await the choice of the Emperor."

Then he added, bowing to Peony, "This maiden is not beautiful, but she looks fat and jolly. My second son is fat and jolly, too. They should do well together if we can arrange matters." (And they were very happy together as it turned out.)

Meanwhile, Spring Breeze was given only an hour in which to get ready.

Peony's mother was, of course, in a rage because Spring Breeze, not Peony, had been chosen. But she forced herself to smile.

"Your sister wishes to make you a gift of some of her dresses," she said sweetly. "You must not disgrace us at court!"

But Spring Breeze thanked her and said she would go in her own simple dress. She would not be at ease in fine clothes. Then she excused herself and ran out into the garden to say good-bye to the lady on the bridge.

"Go, Spring Breeze," the lady said, giving her a camellia flower, "and may your fortune be as good as your heart. We shall not meet again. One thing I ask of you. Wear always in your hair this flower which I have given you."

Day after day Spring Breeze travelled, by boat up the river, on muleback over the mountains, in a palanquin across the valleys, but every morning when she rose, she found the camellia flower as fresh as when the lady had first given it to her.

And so at last Spring Breeze came to the court. Four hundred and ninety-nine beautiful girls were already there. And every one was dressed more beautifully than the last. When Spring Breeze, who was the last to arrive, stood among them in her worn little dress, the other young girls looked at her with surprise. And when they saw that she wore only a flower in her hair, they couldn't believe their eyes.

"What a way to come to court!" they whispered. "The officials should send her home."

But no-one sent Spring Breeze home and the next morning was the day on which the bride for the Emperor's eldest son was to be chosen. It was a beautiful day. Every bird in the palace gardens was singing. The sky was blue. The white clouds were no larger than white water lilies. And in the great courtyard before the palace the young girls gathered in their embroidered robes and jewelled head-dresses like a garden themselves. Each was so splendid that they all looked alike. Only Spring Breeze, in her simple worn robe, with the blossom in her hair, stood out among them.

Suddenly they all bowed down to the ground. The Emperor and his handsome young son had appeared with a crowd of officials at the head of a flight of marble steps.

He smiled at the young girls gathered before him.

"No man," he said, "could choose amid so much beauty. You are like a garden of five hundred flowers. So I have asked for help from a being well acquainted with flowers."

The Emperor gave a sign. An official came forward carrying a small golden cage. And in the golden cage was a large, brightly coloured butterfly.

At a word from the Emperor the door of the cage was opened and out the butterfly flew. It hovered over all the young girls in their jewelled head-dresses, now drifting here, now drifting there, and at last it alighted on the camellia in Spring Breeze's hair.

Then out of the silence, a great shout went up. "The bride has been chosen! The butterfly has chosen the prince's bride!"

So Spring Breeze was married to the Emperor's son among much feasting and rejoicing. And the more that the Emperor saw of his new daughter-in-law the more he praised the butterfly's choice.

"But how is it," he asked her one day, "that living so far from court, you are more accomplished than any of the ladies here? For no one can paint and write a poem, dance, play and sing as well as you."

Then Spring Breeze told the Emperor the story of the lady in the rose-coloured dress who had befriended her. The Emperor listened. And when Spring Breeze was silent, he sat in thought for a long time.

"Do you know who this lady was?" he asked Spring Breeze at last, and when she shook her head, he said, "She was the spirit of the camellia under whose branches you went for comfort. And the old men were the spirits of the pines, and the scholars were the willows. The ladies were the blossoming bushes and the children were the flowers. Such a wonder has not been seen in my time. But I have heard old men say that once in a hundred years the spirits of the garden will appear to a human being who is like themselves. And now I know that your heart is as gentle and as beautiful as your face."

So Spring Breeze lived in the palace beloved by everyone. When at last she became the Empress, she was still as loving and beloved as ever. And still she wore no ornament in her hair but the camellia that the lady in her father's garden had given her so long ago.

The Spirit of the Camellia

When Cricket had finished the story, the Prince clapped his hands with pleasure, and calling him nearer, presented to him with his own hands a small and beautiful lacquered box to hang from his girdle, so that he might always have with him a gift from the descendant of the Sun Goddess.

All the next day the Prince was feeling so well that he was able to observe the routine of the court as he had before he was taken ill, and the land rejoiced, but most of all the Emperor and Empress. When night came the Prince was tired and sent for Cricket who bowed deeply towards the place where the imperial boy was seated, and drawing the magic piece of paper from his breast, read, at the Prince's command, the title of the new story, written in characters fine as the eyebrows of a princess, "The Horse from Nowhere," and then, amid the profound silence of the courtiers, after bowing again towards the Prince he continued.

THE HORSE FROM NOWHERE

Long ago there lived a boy in a house far up on a mountain. It was a lonely place of mists and pine trees, of waterfalls and deer. From the house he could look north almost to the borders of China.

"Beyond lies the desert," his father told him, "where the fierce men of the desert live in their tents. Sometimes they come into China like a swarm of hornets. They ride their shaggy ponies day and night without food or rest. And they kill everyone they meet with."

"Spare us from the swords of the Mongols!" sighed the boy's mother.

"It is many years since they have come," said his father. "Perhaps they have gone far away, herding their mares. Perhaps they will never return. They are like clouds, or the wind."

"What lies over there?" asked the boy, looking towards the south.

His father was silent, but his mother said, "There lies Peking, that great city."

"How far is it away?" asked the boy.

"A long day's ride." It was now his father who answered. "It is better not to think of it. It is nothing to us."

"And we are nothing to Peking," he added to himself, so low that the boy scarcely heard him.

So they lived, looking over peak and valley, fields and villages, far-off temples and yellow rivers. The boy never asked again about what lay to the north and south of them. But he often thought of the desert and the Mongols on their shaggy horses, and of Peking, that great city.

Although there were stables which belonged to the house where the boy lived, there were no horses in them. He did not ask where the horses had gone. There were many questions that he did not ask. Usually he and his father and mother dressed in coarse blue cotton, like the old man and woman who lived with them. They helped carry water from the spring. They worked with the old couple in the garden, to grow food, and his mother's flowers. They were up at dawn, and early to bed.

But on New Year's Day the father and mother were dressed in fine silks, and the dinner was served on beautiful plates. The boy saw everything but he said nothing.

And there were in the house a few beautiful pieces of jade wrapped and put away in a carved box. On rainy days his mother sometimes showed them to him. Now and then, he missed a piece. But he did not ask where it had gone.

There were besides the jade a few other beautiful things in the house. What the boy loved most of all was a painting on a scroll. It showed a black horse, harnessed and bridled, as if ready for his rider. The horse lifted his head impatiently. The wind seemed to stir his long mane. And with one hoof he pawed the ground.

Every morning when he was alone, the boy went to greet the little black horse. It seemed to him that the horse knew him. Did an eye move? Did an ear twitch? The boy could not have said. And yet it seemed to him that every morning the horse greeted him from the scroll on which he was painted.

But one morning the scroll was gone. The boy could not believe it. He looked on all the walls. No, the scroll had not been hung in a different place. He ran, stumbling, to the carved chest. No, the scroll had not been put away with the jade.

He ran to the door. There by the gate his father stood talking with the old man. The old man had his long staff in his hand. He was about to walk down the steep road to the village for supplies. Hours later he would climb back with a load of salt and tea and rice for the household.

It was always after the old man had gone to the village that the boy missed one of the pieces of jade.

Now he ran out to the gate. Carefully wrapped, he saw the scroll in the old man's hand.

"Father," he begged. "Do not send away the little horse! I will eat nothing, almost nothing. I will work before dawn and after dark. I will do anything you wish. But oh do not, do not send away the little black horse!"

His father was surprised. The boy had never told anyone of how much he loved the painted scroll.

"Do not weep," his father said kindly. "The little

horse shall not go. I will send something else in his place. Some day perhaps I shall have to get rid of him, too. But I promise you, he shall be the last of our treasures to go."

So the old man went down the mountain that morning carrying something else in his hand, and the little black horse returned to his place on the wall. But now the boy could not keep silence any longer. He found the old woman working by herself in the garden.

"Tell me," said the boy. "Who are we? Who are you and your husband? Why do we live here? Why do my father and mother sometimes wear cotton and sometimes wear silk? Why does my father turn sad when he speaks of Peking, that great city?"

The old woman put down the short hoe with which she had been working.

"Come, then," she said. "The time has come to speak, since for you the time has come to ask questions. Let us sit down by the spring where we can talk quietly."

When they were seated, she said, "To begin with what is easiest to answer. I was your father's nurse, and the old man is my husband. When all the others left him, he and I remained."

"Why did the others leave him?" asked the boy.

"Your father was a great lord and lived at the Emperor's court at Peking," said the old woman. "More and more the Emperor asked his advice. At last it was only your father's advice that the Emperor wished to hear. Then the other lords became jealous. They, who had been his friends, turned against him. They whispered lies to the Emperor. At first the Emperor paid no heed to them but they went on. A word here, a shrug there, a raised eyebrow somewhere else! They repeated to the Emperor things that your father had said, but not as he had said them.

"So at last the Emperor's heart turned against your father. The other lords wished to have him put to death. But the Emperor would not give the order. So he sent him to this far-away house in exile."

"What is exile?" asked the boy.

"It is to be sent away to a place where one must stay. If your father went down to the village even, his life would not be safe. Only in this house to which the Emperor sent him is your father safe."

So then at last the boy understood everything. And he thanked the old woman. He thanked her for telling him. And he thanked her for her faithfulness to his father.

After that talk the boy often looked towards

Peking, that great city, hidden by a fold of the mountains. And he thought about his father and the Emperor, and the court, and the crowded streets, and the noise and the gaiety. There lay the dust of the world. And there his father and mother and he belonged.

But meanwhile they lived quietly. There was beauty and space around them, but exiles are always a little sad.

One autumn day the boy came into the room where his father and mother sat in the dusk, after a day of work in the garden. She was singing a song which she had made up from her own heart, and as she sang she lightly struck the strings of an instrument which lay across her lap:

> *"The leaves fall,*
> *The cold winds blow,*
> *At night the deer call*
> *In the forests below.*

> *"The stream that so mightily*
> *Bounded with spring,*
> *Has hushed its great song*
> *To a murmuring."*

Then his father took the instrument, and from his heart he answered.

> *"The hawk that sits*
> *In the desolate fells*
> *Is still a hawk*
> *Though he wears no bells,*
>
> *"And the sword is a sword*
> *With a sword's bright will*
> *Though it lie in its scabbard*
> *Dark and still."*

The boy would not have understood what the songs meant before his talk with the old woman. But now he knew that his mother compared his father to an autumn river, quiet and forgotten, and he knew that his father's song meant that his father had not changed, but was the same person he had been at the Emperor's court in the old days.

A great desire to sing a song, too, filled the boy and he, with a bow to his father, took the instrument and sang:

> *"When the nights are cold*
> *Close stand the deer,*
> *And the mice line their nests*
> *As winter draws near.*

Cricket and the Emperor's Son

"When the snow has covered
Flower and fern
In the braziers redly
The fires burn!"

The boy's parents were touched by this last song. A family's love for one another is warmest in bad times, the boy had reminded them. He had said it, too, with beauty.

"Ah, some day you will shine at court!" his mother cried, and then she put her hand to her mouth, and tears filled her eyes. The boy would never be seen at court. Like his father, he would live and die in exile.

Then one evening something happened. Coming in late from cutting wood, the boy saw a far-off band of fire to the north.

"Look, Father," he cried at the door. "What is this?"

His father came out and watched the fire for a little while, shading his eyes with his hand.

"The Mongols have come again," he said. "They are killing and burning as they go. Who will take news to the Emperor? Only we, on our mountaintop, have had the warning."

Running into the house he pulled on his long

leather boots and snatched up a short fur jacket and cap, for the night was cold.

"But if you go into the valley, they will kill you," wept his wife.

"Even so, I must carry the warning," said her husband.

He was gone, and the boy and his mother listened to his footsteps stumbling down the dark mountainside.

"It is his duty," wept the boy's mother, "but oh, I fear that it is his death."

But what was that? There was a whinny from the courtyard and hoofs stamped the cobbles. In the light of the door stood a beautiful black horse with saddle and bridle of scarlet silk. As the boy came near, the horse bent his head.

The boy had never ridden a horse, but he seemed to know just what to do. No sooner was he in the saddle, than the horse had leaped forward into the darkness. But he made nothing of darkness nor of the roughness of the way. Smooth as a swallow in flight, he galloped on, down down down the mountainside. Once he neighed, and a shadow leaped from their path. The boy knew that it was his father, but in vain he tried to pull in his mount. On down the mountain they swept. Through the

sleeping village they thundered and on on on, along the highway now, towards Peking, that great city.

The ride was like a dream. Never did the horse falter in his speed until they halted before the gates of the palace. Torches flared. Officers of the guard ran forward. A messenger hurried to waken the Emperor. And soon the boy was led through seven courtyards, followed by the horse.

There in the last of the seven courtyards, the Emperor stood on a balcony lighted by lanterns. He listened to the boy's tale. Soon troops were pouring out of the city towards the north.

"Now these Mongols will be taught their lesson," said the Emperor. "They will be caught before they can finish their work and escape back into their deserts. But tell me," he added kindly, "who are you, who have saved so many villages?"

Then the boy bowed humbly and told the Emperor his name and his father's name.

"I have been mistaken," said the Emperor. "Only from a loyal father could such a son have sprung. In reward for this night, your father shall be restored again to all his honours. He shall return to my side. Never again shall I listen to lies whispered against him."

So the boy was led away to bed. And his horse was led away to the finest stall in the Emperor's stables. Perhaps the horse slept well. But it was a long time before the boy fell asleep. Over and over in his tired brain he asked himself, "Where have I seen this horse before? And why did he appear out of nowhere to help us?"

But he was tired and at last he fell asleep.

At dawn he woke, and hurried off to see the black horse. But in the stables he was met by confusion and outcry. The grooms had but closed their eyes for a moment's sleep, the cocks had crowed, and when they awoke, blinking in the first light, lo! the black horse was gone!

All day the search went on, but not a single trace of the horse was found. The next day the Emperor ordered one of his finest steeds given to the boy, and he rode home, his heart torn between joy and sorrow. It would be a joy to tell his father that his exile was over. But how could he ever forget his grief at the loss of the black horse?

At last in the late dusk he was home again. The old man led away the Emperor's fine horse to the empty stable. His father and mother rose from their chairs to greet him. All was the same. Even the beloved scroll of the little horse hung in its usual place on the wall.

But suddenly he knew why the black horse which had carried him to Peking had seemed familiar.

There he stood, scarlet saddle, bridle, blowing mane and all!

As the boy told his father and mother all the tale, the old woman listened. At the end she nodded.

"So that was it," she said. "When the young master rode away I happened to lift my candle to the scroll. It was empty. But I was so frightened for the master and the young master, that I said nothing. Still I went back at dawn to make sure. Everything was just as usual. So I thought I must have been dreaming after all."

From that day on, all went well with the boy and his father and mother and the old man and the old woman. They lived in a vast house in Peking, that great city. The father was once more high in the Emperor's favour, and the house was filled with treasures, but the greatest and most honoured of all the treasures was the scroll of silk upon which was painted a little black horse, saddled and bridled and pawing the ground, as though impatient to be off.

When Cricket had finished the last sentence of the tale, he saw with astonishment that the magic page remained blank, and no story appeared upon its surface. Then all knew that the Prince's cure was complete and that the miraculous page had done its appointed work. So the next day the Emperor himself created Cricket a noble of the third rank and gave him apartments and servants in the palace. And furthermore the Emperor and the Empress in their gratitude made him rich gifts, and the Prince never tired of showing *his* gratitude and continued to have him often near him, and the courtiers, instead of being jealous, were so pleased by his modesty and good sense that they vied with one another in becoming his friends.

The first thing that Cricket did was to send for his mother, and together they loved to sit on a balcony overlooking the palace gardens, her hands resting on her silken lap, while she told him one of the stories he used to hear of the snake in the garden, or the foxes, or the wars of the Samurai. She was very proud of him but she said little except once in a while, "I am certain you look as your grandfather looked when he was young," and another time, seeing him on horseback in his fine robes, she said, "it suits you, my son." They understood each other, those two, and her happiness was the greatest honour he won.

For his good fortune never spoiled Cricket, and he did not forget. A few days after he first wore the two swords of a Samurai, he mounted his horse and rode to the temple to see the old priest. He found him in meditation and once more Cricket sat humbly before him and listened respectfully to his wisdom while the doves cooed among the eaves. Then he made him rich gifts and went to offer before the shrine of the God of Writing the magic scroll, incased in a box of precious lacquer, but now blank forever. And there he remained for a long time in prayer.

On the way back to the palace he passed by the shop of his old master, who ran out bowing low and stood beside the stirrup of this new lord who had once been the apprentice he had cuffed about. Perhaps Cricket had an impulse to ride on with a haughty word, but as he had kept himself cheerful and serene in bad days, so he remembered now what was suitable to his own honour. The silk merchant, too, had been all part of his good fortune, even if he had not meant to be. So Cricket looked at him tranquilly and spoke to him with courtesy, ordering a bolt of silk, and so rode on, glad to forget his heavy face creased in false smiles.

And everyone noticed that whenever paper with

writing on it was blown across Cricket's path, he picked it up, even if he had to dismount from his horse in the rain or snow, and took it back to his fine apartments to be burned reverently in an especial brazier. For Cricket was still (and with good reason) as respectful towards the written word, now he was a courtier and a favourite with the throne, as he had been in the old days when he was nothing but a poor apprentice.